RAVEN FEEDER

RAVEN FEEDER

M C Scott

SHORTLIST

This Large Print edition published
2012 by AudioGO Ltd
by arrangement with
Transworld Publishers

ISBN 978 1 4458 2809 1

British Library Cataloguing in Publication Data available

Printed and bound in Great Britain
by MPG Books Group Limited

HISTORICAL NOTES

With the exception of Arne Thoreson, his father and mother, the characters from this story are all taken from the Saga of Olaf Trygvason, and, as such, are as close to being historically accurate as any other characters of the time. Certainly, it appears to be true that Olaf Trygvason was King of Norway in the years leading up to the first millennium, and that he did, unquestionably, convert Orkney by force (and by dint of taking the earl's son hostage), and go on to convert the whole of Norway in like manner. He was killed, finally, in a truly epic sea battle by Eirik Hakonson with the (very limited) aid of the Swedish and Danish fleets. That story in itself deserves retelling, but it is more of an act of extraordinary valour than a crime, and this is not the place.

Instead, I have given Eirik his victory six months early, in time for the millennium, so that he can undo the work done by Trygvason and render northern Europe free of the blight of Christianity for the next thousand years. (One can always dream.)

In the smaller parts, the ship the *Crane* (*Tranen*), was Olaf Trygvason's own flagship, and the largest longship ever seen in northern waters at that period in history. Eyvind Kelda was a Norse 'witch' of Finnish or Lapp decent who was, in fact, tortured to death by Trygvason for failing to accept Christian baptism. I have thus, in my parallel universe, given him a part in the victory. The priest, Thangbrand the Saxon, was, indeed, sent to Iceland, did kill the skald who lampooned him—along with two other men—and then returned to Norway. There is no record of him having been to Orkney, and so his battle with Arne is my invention.

As minor notes of historical detail, remember that the Norse counted in great-hundreds—one great-hundred equals a hundred and twenty—thus a half great-hundred of men is sixty.

Finally, those of you who take part in battle re-enactment will know that the only way to kill a man properly with an axe is with a back-handed cut to the head.

I burned my father at dusk on the day after the summer solstice, in the year nine hundred and ninety nine. I was nineteen years old.

It was not a good day to be building a fire. We were in the aftermath of the worst summer storm the Orkneys had seen in my lifetime. The rain was less than it had been overnight, and the wind had eased from the ear-battering, mind-numbing gale to something where at least we could shout one to the other with a chance of being heard, but it was still not easy to find wood to hold the flame. Because it was my father, the men crossed the island to Kirkwall, which had not seen the worst of the storm, to bring stored timber from the earth houses there, and I used what kindling I found in from the Great Hall at Orphir. Very little of that was dry. Very little of anything anywhere was dry, in the wake of a wind that had lifted the thatch from the rooftops and destroyed three ships on the rocks offshore before we could make fast the fleet. Still, we gathered it in, the wet with the less wet, and over it all we poured oil from the lamps and goose-fat and tallow. Then we laid on ropes from his ship and, lastly, his shield.

I lit the first brand as the sun hit the waves. Fire met fire with the churning water between, and it was as he would have wanted it. We did not fire his own ship. She was the biggest of all our ships: twenty benches, six men to a bench, three men to each sweep, one greathundred of oarsmen to row her forward, and more to man the sails. He had her built in the year of my tenth birthday, and called her *Tranen,*which means the *Crane,* and she was the joy of his life next to my mother, and, I believe, me. In other days we might have fired her for him,

2

but not now when every ship afloat made the difference between losing and winning the war. He would not have wanted that. Instead we used one of the three smaller ships that had part-foundered on the rocks. Twelve of us rowed it into the centre of the current that runs west from Hoy. We used bucket after bucket of water to douse the sail and the rigging, and then half of us left and sat in the small-boat just off the lee side while Einar Sigurdson and I hauled on the rigging and raised the sodden sail. It caught and snapped and billowed, and we jumped clear as the boat bucked once, like a horse newly turned out to grass, and then leapt forward. Last thing before I jumped, I cast the brand that would start the burning, and we followed it with fire arrows for as long as she was in range.

We rowed back to the *Tranen* to watch her go. She was a good ship, and the wind was strong, and she sailed westward towards the sun with nothing to block her path. I stood at the prow and watched the body of Thore, son of Skule, father to Arne, and husband to Ranveig, leader of men and feeder of ravens, burn in a tangle of damp wood to the stench of sheep-fat and goose-grease and a great black sweep of smoke that caught the strength of the salt-wind and surged forward ahead of his boat—so that his last voyage into the sun was down a tunnel of black soot that led all the way to the edge of the world.

I could not have asked for a better omen. In that time, men were talking a great deal about the omens and their meanings. As the Christians counted it, there were a scant six months until their Day of Judgement fell on the land, and they would have every man, woman and child following the new religion— or dead—by that day. That was the measure of Olaf Trygvason's visit to

Orkney; he sailed by chance into the harbour as Sigurd Hlodvirson, Earl of all Orkney, rode out a storm there, and when he sailed out again, Sigurd and—nominally—all of Orkney, were sworn to Christianity. Just to make sure, Trygvason took with him Sigurd's youngest and most favoured son, Hlodvir. The Norwegians named him *Hundi,* which means dog, or *Hvelp,* which means whelp, and is worse, and they held him hostage in perpetuity for the continuing faith of the Orkneys.

That was three years ago, and we were the first. I have thought since that he did not come by chance, that he had heard of my mother and thought to bind her along with Sigurd, and in this way to buy favours from his god. Certainly, it is true that when he left Orkney, Olaf Trygvason sailed straight to Norway and killed the Earl Hakon Eirikson, and had himself made king in his place, so he may have believed that he had pleased his god well. Since then, the new king has spent his summers hunting throughout Norway for all who kept the old way and the old laws—and those who will not convert he takes his pleasure in killing slowly. It is his belief that men can drop the old gods and pick up new ones at his whim, as a skald might pick up a new harp on the word of his master. Some of them do. Some of them don't care, and will do whatever seems politic. The rest of us know that the gods are not changed on the whim of a man, and we wait for their words in the cry of the gull or the flight of the raven—or the sign of a flag of black smoke running to the edge of the world before a ship manned by the dead.

So I spoke, then, with the stench of burning flesh all around us, and the sky twice black with the storm clouds and with the ending of my father. I spoke to Einar Sigurdson who was my closest friend and whose brother languished in Norway, and beyond him I spoke to all the men of the islands who had gathered to honour my father's passing. As I raised my voice, so the wind fell, and the furthest of those gathered on the boats of the fleet or on the shore could hear me. This, too, I counted a gift from the gods.

'Men of Orkney, men of Odin, men of Thor and of Freya, listen to me . . . The Christian priest who builds his church on our islands will tell you that black smoke is a bad omen, a sign that my father will burn for ever in the fires of the Christian hell. This is one of the many things that sets us and him apart. For him, white is good, which is, I believe, because the White Christ comes from the hottest part of the earth, where white is needed to shield them from the midday sun. Here, and in Norway where the true gods lie, white is for ice and for snow, and it is the grey-mawed wolf of winter who takes entire families without pity or mercy. For us, black is of the earth mother, of Frig and the Norns, and is the blessing that guides our nights and our days. The raven is black, he who is the messenger of the gods. The dark earth is black, that feeds us and holds us. The wolf of battle is black, who takes us all in the end. For us, black is the best of signs, as my father was the best of men. Know now that, however he died and whatever was done to him after his death, he has gone to join the true gods in the afterlife, as he deserved.'

It was the longest speech I had ever made in public in my life. I stopped to see how it was taken. All of those present had sailed or fought with my father, and there was a shout of greeting and agreement that made worse the sting of salt in my eyes. It was not a time for grieving, and I think only Einar would have seen that I weakened. I let the sound die with the falling breeze and went on.

'Men of Orkney, you who know my father will know that he never left the true gods. How could he, married to my mother? All of you, who fought with him, know that he was the greatest of fighters, how could he not be, with a ship like the *Crane*?'

Again, and for both of these, the cheer went up. This time I raised my voice above it. 'And so I ask you, any of you, who saw my father with me, to say how he died.'

It was Einar who spoke, as it had to be, because he was the only one with me when we found the body. Einar, my soul-friend, who is first son to Sigurd, and will one day be earl of all Orkney. He came to join me at the prow, beside the head of the *Crane*. He is not as tall as I am, but broader in the shoulders, and where my hair is black of an Icelandish mother, his is the red-brown of a fox in winter, and shone like copper in the evening sun. He has a voice like a bull-horn, and he used it.

9

'Men of Orkney, I will speak now, who was with Arne Thoreson when he found his father. It was this morning, an hour after sunrise, when we were all but done with securing the fleet. Had the night been other than it was, we would have found Thore earlier, and we will each carry the pain of that for the remainder of this life, because his body was still warm in the places where the rain had not cooled it, and the blood still flowed freely from the axe wound that killed him, which means that he had died while we were fighting to save the longships. We had each cursed him for not being there to help us. We will carry that, too.'

He hung his head, and men stood silent, knowing what it does to curse a friend already dead. He lifted his head again.

'I have to tell you what we found. You all knew Thore Skuleson as a man who had never turned his back in battle. This morning, that man

10

lay with his axe never lifted from his belt and his arms by his side and a great wound here'—he brought the heel of his hand to the side of his head, on the left, above the ear—'in the place where an axe struck on the backhand would hit from behind. He was struck only once, and he fell forwards on to his face. This we could tell by the pattern of mud on his skin and his tunic. Then . . .' He paused and gathered himself, and the men leaned forward to hear him better. '. . . then he had been turned over and dragged to a new place, and when he was laid down again, a cross of the White Christ had been placed on his chest.'

He stopped then, because the noise was too great to go on; the noise of men aghast, men in soul-pain, men in anger of the kind that drives battle. Out of it all, came a voice that was pitched to carry. 'Where was he found, Einar Sigurdson? Where did you find him?'

The men grew quiet to hear the answer.

'Not where he fell. There was mud on his heels and his calves from being dragged through the mud. We have searched, and we cannot tell where he fell first; the rain has washed the signs to nothing. All I can say is that he lay finally by the foundations of the Christian church that the Saxon priest is building at Kirkwall.'

The shout that went up then was the shout of a war-host, nothing less. Einar and I stood together in the eye of it, as in the eye of a storm, and felt it hammer our ears and our hearts. I wept then, without shame, and Einar with me. He put his hand on my shoulder. 'There are less of them Christian now than there were this morning,' he said. 'We may have enough now, to sail with us to Norway.' Even then, it was his heart's dream to sail east and take back his brother.

I shook my head. 'If all Orkney was with us, there would still not be enough. And before all else, we must find who killed my father.'

He looked grim, as I must have looked grim, peering eastward through the wind-lashed tears and the after-haze of smoke. 'Is there any doubt?' he asked.

I said, 'There is always doubt until the gods have spoken.' And that was when, in the presence of all the true men of Orkney, a raven flew from the land and, calling, circled three times round the mast-head of the *Tranen*, my father's ship, and then flew east, to Norway. If there was doubt in my mind then, it was answered. The smoke, I had prayed for and then planned for and prayed for again. For the raven, I would not have dared ask.

We rowed the ships to shore, and beached them with care in the face of a possible return of the storm. The men were not to be held, and

13

neither Einar nor I tried to stop them as they ran through the surf and up past the first row of cottages. Sigurd is earl, and he is the one who allowed the Saxon priest to begin building his church, when he knew that he had already killed three men in Iceland for failing to turn themselves to Christ. It was up to Sigurd, then, to decide whose laws to follow—those of the old ways, that say a man is a man and may not be killed unlawfully; or that of Olaf Trygvason, which says that any man who is a Christian may kill any man who is not with impunity. I walked with Einar up the shoreline and we watched four ship-loads of men turn on the Great House and demand word with Sigurd. Einar was pensive. 'They will kill the Saxon.'

'Only if your father permits it.'

'He won't dare turn them down.'

'Then we had best get to your brother before word reaches the Christ-Wolf in Norway that his favourite heathen-slaying priest has gone to meet his god with his head in his hands and a hammer of Thor burning his chest.'

At the door to my mother's house we parted. The last thing I heard as I entered was the odd, high-pitched voice of Thangbrand the Saxon, denying that he had ever killed anyone. And that, at least, was a lie.

*   *   *

I was afraid of my mother. In a different way, I am still afraid of her now, knowing the full measure of what she can do. My mother is a Singer, which gives her more power than any man to know the will of the gods. In the years since then I have travelled to the far north and sat with the reindeer herds, and listened to the beat of their drums, and seen the things that they call out of the smoke of their fires. I have ridden to the east, and spent a winter with the keepers of horses, and slept in the hide of a new-foaled mare, and dreamt the dreams of the all-mother that showed me the ways of the afterlife. But I am not a Singer, and never will be, and I have never met anyone who lived closer to the true gods than my mother. Even Sigurd, with Olaf and his martyred saints on his back, would not presume to convert Ranveig Gunnàrsdottir. He has more sense than that.

I knew nothing of that on the day of my father's burning. I stooped in through the door-skin with the sight of a circling raven filling my mind's eye, and fear turned my legs to water and my water to running wine. I stood with my back to the doorpost, and searched the dark of her home with my eyes. She was there, sitting in the farthest corner with her back to me, watching the colours of her fire. On a night when every other home in Orkney was fighting to find a roof, never mind dry wood to burn, my mother's fire burnt strongly blue, the colour of the morning sky, and then, as I watched, she cast her hand at it, with possibly some powder, and the blue turned to red, the colour of blood in water.

'Is it done as he would have wished it?' Her voice resonated like a struck harp, so that it filled the soul and quenched the fear. I stood straighter.

'Yes.' I stepped forward into the room. 'May I sit?'

'Of course.' She smiled in the dark, so that I could hear the new chord in her voice. Her hands withdrew, and the fire glowed the colour of any fire. 'Was it hard on you?' she asked.

I thought about that, and answered honestly. 'Less than I thought it would be.'

'Good.' She turned so that I could see her face in the firelight, and she was, indeed, smiling. 'Einar looks good with the sun behind him.'

This was one reason we feared my mother. She had not been within sight of the *Tranen* when Einar had spoken. 'He with the sun behind him, you with the moon. Remember that.'

'I will.' I remember everything my mother has said. One day, it may kill me. In the meantime, it has saved my life more times than I can recount. 'Did you send the raven?' I asked.

She shook her head. Her black hair turned red in the light of the fire. Her voice came as if from somewhere else in the room. 'I don't send,' she said. 'I ask.' A cat moved in the far corner, and if you watched closely, you would think the voice came from it. I am used to this. I sat still. She watched things move in the fire. In time, she raised her head. 'You will sail two days from now with Einar, and with the least possible men you can take to sail in safety. Einar's father will stay here, so that if all fails, he can claim no knowledge, and Orkney may be spared the wrath of the Christ-Wolf.' I said nothing. If we took the *Tranen*, lightly manned, we could sail her safely with a half great-hundred men. Sailing was not the problem. It was what we might meet at the other side. Still, I am not one to argue with my mother when she is speaking. The fire glowed low to the coals. Her eyes reflected the colour of it. Her voice flowed in dissonant chords from many places. 'You will berth north of Nidaros. The Wolf will not be there, but you will meet a man called Eyvind Kelda, who will know of your coming. Treat him as you would treat me.'

She turned. Her voice came out of her own mouth. Her eyes picked up the light of the fire and sent it out to me. 'They are asking for you now in the Great Hall. Go—and know that your father did not die in vain.'

*　　*　　*

Only at Yule have I seen so many men, women and children in Orkney's Great Hall as I saw that evening. At a time when every one of them should have been using the last of the light to make fast their homes, they gathered to hear of the death of my father and to judge the man who had killed him. Thangbrand the Saxon is Olaf Trygvason's man. He always has been, and it is true that he was sent to Iceland to bring the people there to Christ, and returned to Norway thrice a killer and with Iceland still for the true gods. That the Wolf sent him next to Orkney says much about the stability of our relations with the Wolf, and everything about the nature of his priest. Thangbrand is a big man, a hand taller than me, and as broad as Einar or his father. He has the wheat-gold hair of the Saxons, but he crops it close across his forehead in the way of the Christian priests.

In the way of his fathers, he wields a Dane axe in battle that has a handle as long as his height, and he can kill a man with the haft on one side and the blade on the other. They had brought his axe with him from his place near the new church, and Sigurd stood with it now, holding it beside him like a standard, a single man standing quiet as the storm raged amongst the people below the dais. It took me a good push and a lot of shouting to fight my way to the front. He saw me as the men thinned out and gestured with his free hand.

'Arne! Come up and talk of what you know.' Einar was there ahead of me, and his father knew as much as either of us, but it was necessary that I tell it again to the crowd.

I vaulted on to the dais and found, behind the earl and the priest, in the darker place where the torches didn't reach, twelve men assembled. This meant they were holding a court in the old way, and that it would be the men, not the earl, who would pass judgement on the Saxon's innocence or guilt. I took a moment to look over them: men who were deemed not to have been tainted by evidence one way or the other, which means, in this case, that they were neither for the old gods nor the new, and that they had not seen the wound on the body of my father. In the former there was more difficulty than the latter; we had called for four men to help us carry his body back to my mother, but most of those who had helped build the pyre had seen him lying in state on his shield after she had done dressing him in his war gear. The presence of his helmet on his head meant that the killing wound was not readily seen. Thus the men had not been tainted by the evidence in the way that they would be by their vows. Running my eye along the line, I saw that Sigurd had chosen six who had turned to the White Christ, and six who still spoke for the gods. It was the only thing he could do.

When I turned back, he was waiting for me. He had given the war-axe to Einar, and held the Bible in one hand and the hammer in the other. Now, he offered both to me without a word. I took the hammer. The priest turned away and spat.

Sigurd held up his hand for silence, his eyes on me. 'Tell us,' he said. 'Speak the truth as you know it.'

And so I did. Before they had heard it from Einar, now they heard it, not much different, from me; a brief recital of the moment when we found my father. It didn't take long. I was heard through in silence. At the end, Sigurd turned to the twelve. 'Does anyone amongst you wish to question this man?'

None did. It was not as if they were hearing anything new.

Sigurd turned to the priest. 'Thangbrand the Christian. Give account of yourself. Where were you last night?'

The priest was more angry than I have ever seen him. More so than when my father and I refused to take on the White Christ. His face was blotched red and white in uneven patches. His veins stood out as if carved on the rock of his temples and neck. He said nothing. Sigurd asked it again. In the old laws, a question asked three times and not answered is a sign of guilt. The man knew this. Sigurd waited. Where before there had been a hum of voices, now there was silence. The wind soughed through the cracks in the walls. The torches crackled. A dog, left outside, scratched at the door to come in. All else was quiet.

In the length of the quiet, Sigurd asked it the third time. His voice rang off the walls.

The Saxon took a breath. He was more white now than red. He lifted the Bible from Sigurd's hand and held it up. 'I was asleep,' he said.

24

The silence became a wall. Sigurd said, 'The roof came off half the homes in Orkney last night. Doors were wrenched from their hinges. We lost three boats of the fleet. No living being could sleep through a storm such as that.'

The Bible shook in the Saxon's hand. 'I would not lie on Christ's Bible. I tell you again, I slept from my evening meal until long after daybreak. I was not awake when the heathen died. '

'So then can you kill in your sleep?' That was Einar, and he spoke out of turn, but no man there would have stopped him.

Sigurd looked around the hall. 'Did any man or woman here see the Saxon during the night?'

The wall pressed in. Harald Half-hand raised his stumped arm. 'I knocked on his door to ask for help as the storm was at its height, and got no answer. I thought him already out. I did not think to go in and see if he slept.'

Sigurd turned back to the man at his side. His brows met together in the centre of his forehead. 'How could you sleep through that?' I think he was genuinely puzzled.

The Saxon lowered his book. 'Ask the witch's son. The roof came off my cottage as it did all the others except for his mother's. I woke this morning as wet as if I had been down to the floor of the Pentland Firth. And yet I did sleep. Ask Arne, son of Ranveig, how this could be so. I know nothing of witchcraft. I am a mere man of god.'

He might have drawn them to his side then, had he not said that last thing. Not the accusation of witchery—my mother is a witch and proud of it—and I would not put it past my mother to make a man sleep through his own burning if needs be, nor to call up a storm to cover it. There were others who might have believed as much, even if they would not believe she would set a man to kill her own husband. But the Saxon was no *mere* anything, and he was known to have killed in the name of his god. In that he made his mistake. The wall that had been holding the voices broke, as a dam breaks before the melting snow, and the noise was the same as that on the ships when my father burned, only contained by the Great Hall as in a vessel of sound.

Sigurd rode it as he would ride a ship in a storm. When the calm came, he spoke again to the Saxon.

'Thangbrand, favoured of Olaf Trygvason. Do you deny that you threatened Thore Skuleson and his family with the wrath of the White Christ for failing to take your baptism?'

'For failing to take *Christ's* baptism. I am the intermediary, not the son of god. No, I do not deny it.'

'And do you deny having called down the wrath of your Christ, with the aid of your Dane axe, on Thorvald Veile, and Veterlide the skald, and one other man while in Iceland?'

'I do not deny it. They, too, refused the baptism of the White Christ.' They had done more than that. Veterlide had composed ten long verses relating what he thought of Thangbrand and his new god. It was for that he had died, but men sing the verses still in all the lands of the north.

Sigurd took the hammer from my hand and gave it to his son. He turned me round to face the front of the hall. Einar, he turned to face the back. 'Einar Sigurdson will bring the charge,' he said. It was not for me, as the blood relative, to seek to charge the facts with my anger.

The twelve men sat still at the back of the dais. In all of this, they had remained calm. Einar used his voice as he had used it on the ship, so that it carried back to the far end of the hall behind him.

'Men of the Orkneys. We all knew Thore Skuleson, and we could sing songs in his honour. Now is not the time for that. In this, there are only two things that matter. First that Thore, though a great man, no longer had ears as sharp as they had been. All of you will have known how often he had to ask twice when you bade him good morning.' They nodded at that, and some smiled. My father's encroaching deafness had been a source of constant comment from his peers, as is every failing sense in those growing old.

Einar went on. 'The other thing beyond question is that he was a warrior born, and no man would have bested him had he the mind to defend himself.' They nodded for that, too, and it was true. 'Therefore I bring this charge before you: that Thangbrand the Saxon, in the darkest and hardest part of the storm, did come upon

Thore Skuleson in stealth, and did take his life from him, using the coward's blow from behind—against a man who could not hear his enemy coming, and so did nothing to defend himself. I ask, therefore, in accordance with the old laws and those of the Bible, that we take an eye for an eye and a life for a life—I say that the Saxon has forfeited his right to live.'

It is not given for the men on the floor to influence the assembly. Still, the groundswell was with him.

Sigurd turned and lifted the Bible in the Saxon's hand. 'You may make your plea,' he said.

Nobody has said that the Saxon was not a brave man. He held the Bible high, and his voice carried every bit as far as Einar's. 'I swear before Almighty God that I slept through the night, and that I did not take a hand in the killing of Thore Skuleson. I have killed before. God willing, I will kill in his name again.

But not this time.'

He lowered his book. 'Nevertheless, I have no proof of this if you will not take my oath on the Bible. Therefore I offer a decision in the old ways. I will fight Arne, son of Thore, in single combat, and let my god and his show who is speaking the truth here.'

Men drew breath at that. It was a clever move. Without that, he was a dead man. With it, either one of us could have been. But I had the black smoke and the raven, and the words of my mother rang in my ears. More, I had a full moon rising in the black sky above Orphir. I stepped forward and took the hammer again from Einar.

'I accept your offer.' I heard the echo of my words come back from both walls. 'There are men here who need to be tending their homes and their families. Let it be done now, under the light of the moon, before the storm returns to harry the fleet further.'

He was thirty-four years old, and a man in his prime who had killed beyond counting. I was three days after my nineteenth birthday, and it was well known that I had not yet taken my first man in battle. For the rest of my life I will remember the size of his smile.

*   *   *

There are rules for these things, but not all of them are rigid. Einar was the one to suggest that, because we were both skilled with the axe but the Saxon had the longer reach, it would be more even if we fought with the sword, with which we were both less familiar. I would have thought the priest would have turned that down, but he accepted it, as he accepted other things one would not have thought of him. Later, my mother told me he had been raised in the horse herds to the east, and had lived with their customs, which are not unlike ours, before he ever came north to be the long arm of Christ's Wolf in Norway.

It was a cold, clear night with almost no wind: a poor night for sailing, but the best of all possible nights for fighting. The moon was part-risen above the Great Hall's roof-ridge, and it lit to daylight the flat ground they chose for us to the west of the hall. Beyond the land, the water lay quiet after the chaos of the storm, and the first sliver of moonlight slid across it as milk across a floor. The ground itself was flat and smooth from years of threshing corn, and most of the stones had been taken out long ago. Those that had not stuck proud from the ground, and their shadows lay crisp to the side of them, so that there was no danger one might stub a toe and loose footing. I stood at the northern end of it, as was my birthright, and had Einar bind the lengths of boiled leather around my forearms and calves, and another around my brow to make tight the fit of my helmet. I raised my arms above my head, and he lowered the chain mail over them, so that it settled on my shoulders and hung part-way to my knees. He tied my belt to my waist, and slid into it the haft of the small throwing axe that had been allowed as the second weapon. If we had been going to battle, he would have brought me my shield, and then I would have dressed him likewise. As it was, the gods and their truth were our shield, and there was no need for Einar to dress in any way other than he already was.

Sigurd stood in the centre of the field. When I was ready, I walked to him. The Saxon joined us from the south side. As we met in the centre, the moon rose clear of the roof-ridge so that the light of it painted a single stream out across the oil-flat water, and the voice of my mother rang in my head. *'He with the sun behind him, you with the moon. Remember that.'* How could I forget? And then the cry of the raven filled my ears, and I looked up, which was pointless, because ravens do not fly at night, and yet on this night, one did, flying up the silver line of the moon, heading east for Norway. It called three times as it passed overhead, and when the noise died down, Sigurd stepped back into safety.

You will know of battle. In the moments before, it is good to hear the war-cry of the host, and to feel the bodies of one's companions on either side. In single combat it is different: then there is only the beat of the heart, not the beat of the drums; the cry of the sinews as they move into action, not the cry of other men. There is the taste of metal in the mouth, and the churning of guts, and the moment of coming to terms with the single man who will kill you if you do not kill him first. A full battle is about seeing before you are seen. Single combat is about believing. At the moment when I believe I am going to die, then I will do so. On this night, I stepped forward under the light of the full moon, with the cry of the raven in my ears, and for one long moment, Thangbrand the Saxon shrank before me to the size of a child. Still, a child may kill if it chooses, and when he launched the first blow it was with the strength of a full-grown man against a nineteen-year-old youth, and I knew that whatever my mother had said, I could die as easily as had my father. I blocked the blow, and cut down towards his knees—so that he jumped back to give me space. Still striking, I stepped sideways three steps, to put my back to the west and hold the light of the full moon behind me. The Saxon paced with me, eastwards, to put his back to the sea. The light shone on his sword, marking out the Christ's cross engraved on the blade. Mine stayed black in the shadow. I sought his eyes. In the light of the sun, they were grey. In the moonlight, they were clear, as if looking down a tunnel, and quite empty of feeling. In battle, one cannot afford to feel. His sword came at my head, at the height of my ears. I ducked and struck forward and then pulled my blade urgently sideways, just in time to block the full impact of his back-swing. The shock of it made my teeth clash on my tongue, and I tasted blood. I jerked the short-axe from my belt and re-gripped my sword one-handed, to give me use of both weapons. His blade swung in a double loop, twisting in the centre, so that any of four cuts could have killed. I took two of them on my blade, and one on the axe, and the last I let swing clear to pull him off balance before I threw my own attack at his knees, his chest, his skull, his elbows. Not one of them made contact with anything, but steel and the force of it spun us both to the edges of the clearing to take breath and come in again.

I have no idea how long we fought. Time drew down to the end of a blade and the small edge of a hand-axe. We both drew blood, neither of us badly. We both tasted salt and iron and the acid of exhaustion. We both tired, but equally, so that one was not slower than the other. Around us, the men, women and children of Orkney stood in silence, giving us due respect—all bar my mother who watched it in her fire.

It was she who made the difference, in the end. The Saxon made a half-feint to my knees, and brought his blade up at a sharper angle than he had done before, aiming for a cut to the thigh on the back-stroke. I brought my sword-hand down to block it, and, as the blades screamed on the strength of his stroke, the light of the moon caught on both and was blinding. I jumped back out of reach and looked upwards. The moon was very close to being straight overhead. My mother spoke in my ears as she had done before. *'The moon behind you. Remember that.'* Behind. Not above, or in front. I thought she had been warning me to keep clear of the sun, or to watch Einar if he took to battle in darkness. It had not occurred to me that, instead, she had been telling me to kill before the moon reached its height.

The Saxon had taken pause to breathe and to think. I looked again at the moon and let the whole understanding of it show on my face. He saw it, and did not understand, but he was weary and his wits were not as sharp as they had been at the start, and he looked to the moon anyway, to see what I had seen. In that was his death. It is said that Olaf

Trygvason can kill two men at once with a spear thrown from each hand. I use my sword in my left hand and have done so since birth—I am, after all, a witch's son. But I am also the son of my father, and I can throw my hand-axe with either hand. I used both, then. The hand-axe aimed for his head, the sword sliced in a killing arc a hand's breadth down from his neck. He saw the first and ducked. He could not have seen the second. With a shock down my arm that was quite different from the clash of iron meeting iron, my blade bit in the gap between his helmet and his mail, and hewed into his neck. I did not take off his head—the only man on the island with the strength to sever that head was the man on whose shoulders it rested—but the length of my blade cut across the full width of his throat, and his life flowed in its wake. He was dead before I finished the stroke. Dead, and, by extension, guilty.

* * *

I remember nothing of the hours
that followed. I woke in my mother's
home, lying in a shard of broken
sunlight with a cat asleep on my
chest. There was a cat-skin pouch on
my belt, and a bandage replacing the
boiled leather on my left forearm,
and the smell of groundwort and
pig's fat came from beneath it.
Something else burned on the fire
and turned the air sweet. A raven
with a single white feather in each
wing sat on the roof beam and
watched me, or the cat, or both. I
tried to remember if the ravens I
had seen after the burning of the
Tranen, and before the fight with
Thangbrand had had white feathers,
but they had flown too high and too
fast to know. My mother moved from
her place at the foot of the bed to a

place where I could see her smile. 'Welcome back,' she said.

I tried to sit up and she stopped me. 'Not yet, hound of my hearth. You are not all the way back yet.'

'Where have I been?'

She smiled. Her eyes were violet, beneath hair the colour of the raven, with a white streak at the crown that I had not seen before. Her skin was perfect. I have no idea how old she was. 'I don't know,' she said. 'I was hoping you could tell me.'

I lay back and looked at the cat. The cat looked at me. It stuck up one hind leg and washed the curve of its flank. I closed my eyes and brought back the dream. 'I was running,' I said. 'In Nidaros. There was a man with black hair and a white streak like yours. He flew ahead of me.'

'How did he fly?'

'He used his drum to carry his spirit. He flew to the lair of the Christ-Wolf, where he keeps Einar's brother. He brought me back a token of his hair.'

My mother was kneeling by my side. Her smile was the smile a mother gives to a child who, in learning to walk, has taken the full width of the room and is ready for more. 'Let me see it,' she said.

I opened my left hand, my sword hand. A single red-gold hair lay across it, that could have been the Saxon's. Then, I chose to believe that it was. My mother lifted it with great care and carried it back to her place by the fire. I saw the flames burn black and an oiled green, the colour of a magpie's back. I saw a man's face in the flames, and then blood. 'The man with the badger-striped hair was Eyvind Kelda,' she said, and it was as if the name had been part of me since my youngest days. 'He is waiting for you as I said he would be. You will go to take back Hlodvir, Einar's brother. He will help you in this. In return, you will help him as he asks you.'

She was right, he was waiting for us. At the end of the crossing, with the *Tranen* lightly manned and Einar Sigurdson alone at the helm, we rowed at dusk into an inlet three hours march north of Nidaros, and beached the ship. On the shore, sitting by a fire built of driftwood with a flame that burned clear, like amber, and gave no smoke, was the man I had seen in my mother's fire. He stood as we beached the boat and came to help us. Close up, he was lean, and as tall as me. His hair was dark red, with the white flash at the temples, as mine has now. His face was lean, and there were scars on his cheeks, balanced one side for the other. None of that, in itself, was what set him apart. More, it was the way he stood and the stillness he held with him, such as my mother holds with her, and the sense that here was someone who walked with the gods. It was the first time I had met a man of power. It was, in fact, the first time I had met anyone of power who was not my mother. I stepped forward out of the surf and waved. He left his fire and came down to the waterline to greet us.

'Welcome, hound of the hearth.' It was the second time I had heard that name. 'You made good time.'

'We had the gods behind us.' I looked past him to the dark beyond the fire, and the two figures sitting quiet beside it. I had not been expecting company. 'You are not alone?'

'No.' He turned and gestured. The first man rose and came to join us. Behind me, men reached for their weapons. The newcomer was, if anything, built bigger than the Saxon. In his favour was the fact that his hair reached to his shoulders and was braided for battle, and he wore the hammer at his chest, not the cross of the Christians. In that moment, I would have said he was as unhappy to see us as we were to see him. His face was florid, and not from the heat of the fire.

'You promised me an army, Kelda,' he said. ' Not a bare handful of men.' We were a half great-hundred, which is more than a handful, but we were not an army by any means.

The lean man stretched a palm to him and stillness flowed from it. 'Sometimes a handful can achieve more than an army,' he said. 'And it is only one man who must die.'

Weapons moved further in their sheaths. Einar stepped forward, and the three-quarter moon shone on his blade. 'We are here to take back my brother. We kill who stops us. If none get in the way, none will die.'

The witch-man smiled in the way my mother smiles at a cat. 'Einar

Sigurdson, do you think if you take back your brother tonight and Olaf Trygvason lives, that the Orkneys will be a safe place to hide?'

Einar watched him. We had thought of that. Olaf Trygvason was not kind to those who angered him. Any man might die in battle. None of us wished to die on a cross or a wheel, and we had word that a man could be made to live in agony for three days if the Christ-Wolf set his mind to it. Nevertheless, my mother had said that we would take Hlodvir safely, and that Orkney would not be assaulted. We trusted her words. Einar turned to me. In this, I had his trust also. 'Arne?'

I looked at the giant standing between me and the fire, and knew where I had seen his double before. 'You are Eirik, son of Hakon, who was Earl of Norway. Am I right?'

The blond man said nothing, which was his right. Word had had it he was in Sweden. Olaf Trygvason had spent

47

a fortune on envoys to Sweden in an attempt to buy his life. If Eirik was taken alive in Norway, three days would be the start of his dying. He looked at me, and the truth was in his eyes. Eyvind Kelda let us talk that way in silence, and then he gestured again to the fire and the second man came to join us, and any need for talking was done. Einar's blade slammed home in its sheath.

'Hlodvir! How are you here?' He was right, it was his brother. A small, lean, neat, darker version of Einar, with his hair cut in the Norwegian style. Einar grasped him by the shoulders. 'Are you well?'

'I am. I will be better when I see the hall at Orphir, but I am well enough now.' His voice was not as clear as it had been when he was younger. As he moved in the firelight, it could be seen that he was tired and not well fed, and more than a little drunk. Above all of that, he had not fought for three years, and it showed.

I asked again the question Einar had put to him. 'How are you here?' I asked.

'I was at Nidaros,' he said. 'The king is not there. He has gone inland to Magnus Grenske's farm. I stayed in Nidarholm with the lower half of the court. Eyvind Kelda and the earl-son came in disguise, and freed me as the moon rose this evening.' He looked to each of the men he had just mentioned. When neither spoke, he said, 'If I am not back by morning, my loss will be noticed.'

And so that was it. My mother had said I would do for Eyvind Kelda that which he asked of me, and I had listened and nodded and assumed something small. I had not considered that he might want us to take the throne for the next Earl of Norway. I forget, even now, that when my mother says something will happen, she is not giving an order, but stating the truth—and that she does not deal in small things. We stood on the beach with the men at our back and said nothing. We had Hlodvir, and we could have sailed, but there was none who believed we could face the entire fleet of Norway, even had all of Orkney been with us. On the other hand, there was none who believed that a half great-hundred of men could take the kingship and give it to the earl-son. In time, Einar looked at the two men who flanked his brother. He said, 'You believe this can be done?'

The witch-man raised his hands and gestured back towards his fire. 'Shall we sit?' he said.

*   *   *

We sat for an hour, maybe slightly less, by the fire on the beach. Less than five minutes of that was spent deciding *if* we would do it. The rest was devoted to how. It was not complicated; the best plans never are. As in all cases where a smaller force assaults a larger one, we had the advantage of surprise: of the dark, and of not having spent half the night and all of the week before it drinking ourselves to a stupor. We also had the advantage of being in the open, while the Christ-Wolf and all his men were sleeping in a wooden farmhouse in the height of midsummer—when wood burns like dried grass. It is an easy way to kill, and has little valour in it, but we were not there for honour or glory, we were there for vengeance and to put a man on the throne—and we intended to live to see it happen.

In the end it was settled. Twelve men stayed with the *Tranen* to guard her from sea-ward attack. The rest of us picked up our weapons and gathered in three groups, and followed the witch-man, the earl-son and Einar's brother as, together, they led us inland.

It was an hour's march to the steading. I watched Einar and Eirik leaving at the head of the first group. Whatever their misgivings, they had put them aside, and they walked together as if they had been born from the same womb. They suited each other and they knew it; both big men with an earldom as their birthright, who knew what it was to lead men in battle. This is the thing that makes bonds between countries that last for a lifetime, and that don't fall apart at the first offer of men or money or land. I touched my hammer and gave a prayer that it would last. Hlodvir took the middle group. He was not fit for battle, but he would not have it said that on the night of his rescue he stayed with the ship, and he knew the way to the steading; there was that much in his favour.

I walked with the third group and took the rearguard, as was my right.

Eyvind Kelda chose to walk beside me.

'Are you well, son of the she-hound?' I had not then heard my mother so named. In another man's mouth, it would have been an insult for which one us would have died. In the north, where Eyvind Kelda comes from, the hound is a man's closest companion, and the protector of his soul. The knowledge of that kept my hand from my axe.

I nodded. 'I am well.'

'Einar Sigurdson is a good man,' he said. 'He thinks well.' Listening to him was like watching knife blades glide over ice: everything slid in harmony and was beautiful, but it was things he did not say that hung in the air around him. I watched them now, and waited for him to speak them.

'You think it cannot be done,' I said, when he had walked beside me for a while in silence.

He gave the smile that I was

coming to know as assent. 'I know it cannot be done the way he thinks it,' he said. He had just spent an hour helping Einar and Eirik to plan otherwise.

Still, I believed him. I said, 'Then how?'

His eyes looked into mine. They were black, and things moved through them like flames from his driftwood fire. 'What did you bring me from your mother?' he asked.

The cat-skin pouch—of the kind she uses to keep her sacred things in—still hung from my belt. I had forgotten, to be honest, that I carried it. I unhooked it now, and passed it to the witch-man, who weighed it before he opened it. He was pleased with what lay inside.

'Good.' He put his hand to my arm. 'Then, when we reach the clearing at the Grenske steading, tell Einar to hold his men and let us work first. He will take it better from you than from me.'

*   *   *

In that, as in most things, he spoke only half the truth. Einar took it from me as he might have taken a hive full of bees. He would not have taken it from the witch-man at all. Like most of us, he was able to turn a blind eye to the witch-mist that enshrouded our men and let us walk through the night. It was something else entirely to be asked to stand in silence under a three-quarter moon within bow-shot of his sworn enemy and do nothing. That the men did so when Einar asked it is testament to his leadership and the honour in which they held him. That he asked it of them at all was his gift to me. Eirik Hakonson, who owed nothing to anybody, would have killed all three of us had it not been that we were too close to risk the noise.

What changed him was when Eyvind led us through the trees to within sight of the steading to show us more clearly what we faced. I lay beside the earl-son with my face buried in pine-loam beneath the shadows of the first rank of trees, and saw the light of the moon reflect back at us from the wood of the farmhouse as it would from a polished blade. Wood doesn't shine like that, not unless it's been underwater. To push the point home, the wind backed round on us then, and the earthen smell of sodden timber blew back on the breeze. Eirik cursed in the name of every one of the gods, and when he was done he drew a knife faster than any could have stopped him and held it to Eyvind Kelda's throat.

'He has soaked it, witch-man. He knows we are coming, and he has soaked it so that it cannot burn. You will die before I do. I promise you that.'

Kelda smiled his cat-smile and

kept his neck still. 'I will die before you do, anyway,' he said, 'But not tonight.' He pushed the blade-hand away. 'The king is not stupid. These things should not surprise you. Remember it for later, when you are in his place—better to sleep damp and have the serfs hunting far abroad for firewood, than to die cooked in your own bed.'

'So how do we do it? You would have me call him out and fight him single-handed?'

'Not unless you want to die before the gods would take you, no.' He turned and slid back along the way we had come. For a lank man, there was little enough to hear of his passing. Back at the men, he had us sit. 'You wanted fire,' he said. 'I will give it to you. Have your men place their timber as you planned. Call me as the dog-fox barks when it is done.'

It is astonishing, sometimes, what men will do if they trust enough. Each of us had gathered and cut timber along the way. A half great-hundred, minus twelve, with two extra, is fifty men, fully laden. It is enough fuel to burn down the best of houses, but still some of those who placed theirs earliest went back into the forest for more. We worked quickly, and in silence, and if there were dogs in there, they were as drunk as their masters. At the end of it, brushwood and bigger timber was piled three feet high around the full circuit of the farmhouse, with deeper, denser piles at the doors and windows. Still, it was not the driest of wood, and the farmhouse itself ran with water, as the sails of my father's ship had run before we set fire to it. Given pitch and sheep-fat and goose-oil, we might have fired it alone, but we had none of those things, and nor, as far as I could tell, had Eyvind Kelda.

We stepped back and gathered at the wood's edge, and Eirik Hakonson, smiling as a man smiles at his own death knell, made the bark of a dog-fox to its vixen.

The witch-man joined us in seconds. The earl-son said nothing, simply nodded once to the man and once to the steading. Einar was less restrained. 'We have done our part,' he said. 'We are waiting for you to do yours.'

'Good.' Eyvind Kelda looked past Einar to where I was standing with the earl-son. 'We will need six fire arrows,' he said.

I knelt to find the steel and tinder. A shadow fell across my hand. The witch-man tapped me on the shoulder. 'Not you,' he said. 'I need you with me.'

I had not expected that. I had my axe at my side and my mind half-set for battle. Staring at him, I felt the smooth grip of the haft. 'I know no magic.'

'I know.' He didn't smile. 'But you are the son of your mother. It is not possible to do it without.'

I might still have refused, but Einar stepped back and knelt beside me. 'I have tinder,' he said. 'We will make the arrows and light them. Go with the witch.' I had no choice. I went.

Eyvind Kelda led me round the back, into the shadow where the moonlight lit least. We stood in black silence. I could smell fresh-cut wood and wet timber and cat from the skin my mother had sent him. The witch-man kept his hand on my shoulder and put his mouth close to my ear. 'How well can you recall your mother?' he asked. I shrugged. We were too close to the enemy to risk speaking. Still, he nodded as if I had answered.

'Think of her now. Think of her fire as you last saw it, with her sitting beside it.'

The hairs rose at the back of my head. I am used to my mother speaking like that. Not other men. He moved his grip to my arm, and moved me forwards, sun-wise around the back of the building. He spoke to me in a language I did not understand, and I heard the voice of my mother inside my head. She said, *'Do it now.'*

We walked very slowly side by side, he closer to the walls, me closer to the edge of the clearing. At the beginning, all I could hear was the sound of our feet on the packed earth, and it sounded like a host gearing up for battle, and there was no way the Christ-Wolf would not hear it and wake. Soon, with the witch-man's grip on my arm, and the sound of his voice speaking nonsense in one ear and my mother speaking clearly in the other, I let go of the fear of discovery and imagined myself a child again at my mother's hearth, with the flames burning gold and then rose. I saw the cat come in from the rain, dripping wet, and sit at the fire to dry itself, growling low in its throat, as they do when the hunt has been good.

Gradually, as we came round into the moon, the stink of wet cat became less than it had been, and I could smell clean fur, and dry wool, and hear the voice of my mother singing the songs of her childhood about hearth-fires and their burning. Later, a man told me we walked round three times. I only remember it as once. Whichever it was, we returned to the place we had come from, and I felt the grip grow less on my arm. I was not aware of the pain of it. In battle, one never is. Still, even now, I could show you the burn marks where the witch-man held me. At the time, I stood in the half-dark under a waning moon and saw a man who had aged ten years stand before me. There was more white at his temples than there had been. If he was a raven when we started our circuit, he was a magpie when we finished. The smooth tan of his face had become grey-yellow and his scars stood out white. 'Thank you,' he said, and his voice was thinner, but it still made my hair rise. 'Now you can fight.'

*   *   *

There is too much to tell you of the battle that followed. You need to know that the wood burned as if we had dried it in a kiln, and the steading with it. We ringed it in steel, one man deep all the way round, two deep at the doors and the windows. Olaf Trygvason was not the first to come out. My guess is that he had drunk more than some of those closest to the door, and that perhaps men did not have waking their king as their first thought when they smelled smoke and saw flames and heard the sounds of death all around them. Then, when he did come at last, it was not alone, for he had his bondsmen and his bodyguard around him, and all of them had sworn on their new god—as we would have done on ours—to die before him. There were a dozen of them, maybe more. They held rugs soaked in water before them, and threw a bucket on the flames by the door as they came. Already the walls were ablaze, and the roof timbers were falling, so the splash of wet did little to put out the flames—but it made a great deal of smoke and hid at first who was coming. It was Hlodvir, the hostage, who had seen him most recently, who called out the name. I heard his voice as the cry of a gull in the storm of battle.

'Trygvason! There! The red tunic and the helm in the middle of the bondsmen.'

There were four of us fighting together: me and Einar, Eirik Hakonson and Hlodvir. Behind us, Harald and Thorlief Egilson and Skeggi Hoskuldson fought in a three-pointed star. So seven of us faced twelve, with the king in the middle. We came together in a curving line, shield and axe together. They had only axes and one sword amongst them, and only the king wore a helmet. Four of his bodyguard were known to fight bare-sark for preference. They stood to the fore, axes swinging and began their death-song. Looking back now, they were not calling on the White Christ. At the time, one does not notice these things. There was one to the left with hair almost white and a great burn mark down his left arm. I took him first with my throwing axe—a deep wound to the chest– and then followed it up, from the side, with my great-axe. At the other side, an archer took another. Einar and Eirik Hakonson picked one each and began fighting, which was when the king saw who they were.

If Einar has a voice like a bull-horn, Olaf Trygvason can call on the voice of the thunder-god himself. He raised his head, and the noise of it would have carried all the way to Nidaros. 'Treachery!' he bellowed, which was obvious, and then 'Orkney and Hakonson!' which, perhaps, was not.

Nobody has ever said that the Christ-Wolf could not fight. He took the kingship by force, and he held it by force and it was his axe-arm men feared most. We were seven facing eight when he threw his helmet at Einar and lifted his great-axe, which was bigger than the Saxon priest's had ever been, and began the howling swing of a true berserker. No man stands before that and expects to live. Skeggi Hoskuldson died in a bright splash of blood as his face caught the full force of the first swing. Later, we identified him by the ring on his arm. Thorlief Egilson and his brother cast axes from either side, before Harald died where he stood. Blood flowed like running water, and behind us, a building made of itself a pyre that burned metal as if it were straw. In all the sounds of screaming men and falling timber, I heard my name.

'Arne! Look to Eirik!' It was Einar, fighting on the far side of the group now, killing one of the bondsmen with the back edge of his sword-blade, swinging for another. The three-quarter moon shone clear over his right shoulder.

'Einar. Move out of the moon!' I screamed it as I have never screamed anything else, and I was too late. The king swung to the sound of his voice saying the name of the one man he feared above all. The great mallet of his axe came down in an arc that started up at the height of the moon and finished at the ground, and it passed through the chest of Einar Sigurdson, my soul-friend, in the middle. I was not sane then.

'*Einar!*' I caught up the blade of a bare-sark and threw it wide. A man moved on my right. Ahead of me, the killing axe, fresh with red blood and bone, swung back in its arc. I hurled all that I had forward in to meet it, and struck with my axe in a back-handed stroke for the helmet-less head, for the bright-gold hair, for the black eyes of the Christ-Wolf—and saw them all showered in red before a hand reached in and tore the breath from my throat and the life from my heart and left me falling through eternity to a floor that wasn't there.

I woke to the grey light of dawn with a man leaning over me. It was Eirik Hakonson, earl-son, now King of all Norway. He was stripped to the waist, with great burn marks over the skin of his chest and his shoulders, and the hair burnt all away from his back. His face was red and white in patches, and a purpled bruise swelled his upper lip. 'Einar?' I asked.

'I'm sorry.' He reached down and gripped my forearm. 'If you can stand, I would show you him before he goes to the gods.'

I could stand. I could also walk and look around me and recognize the living, and count the bodies of the dead. 'Eyvind?'

'He lives. And Hlodvir. Orkney will have its earl when Sigurd goes.'

'It will not be the same.'

'No. It will not be the same.'

We came to the pyre. It was bigger than my father's, although it was on land and not at the sea. We had no boat to spare, and Eirik was not prepared to start asking for things until he had secured himself in the kingship. Still, they had given Einar Sigurdson everything a warrior can ask for. He lay in peace on his shield, in full armour, with his sword and his axe at his side, and they had gathered as much wood for this one man as we had gathered to burn the entire steading. There was a reason for that. When I looked further, I saw that it was a pyre for two. Or, perhaps, there was one and then a smaller one behind it. I looked at Eirik.

'Trygvason.' He spoke it as a minor curse; a small withered thing of no consequence. Then he tapped my shoulder. 'Come. You killed him. You should see it.'

They had done him no honour. He lay naked on bare wood, with no armour and no weapons. I am told this is how the Christians would have it, but I doubt if it was done with that in mind. He was burned far more badly than any of the living. His skin was blistered all along one shoulder, turning to black at the elbow, as if he had tried to force his way through the fire at another point before he came to the door. The wound on his head was a good one: clean and sharp. It bit deep, like my father's. He was only the fourth man I had killed.

Eirik Hakonson leant on the side of the pyre. 'Einar told me of your fight with the Saxon,' he said. 'If you ever feel you want to leave Orkney, there will be a place for you in Norway. I will need a bodyguard of men who can kill with weapons they do not favour, along with those that they do.'

I nodded. It was not a time to think of such things. The king reached forward and traced the wound on the Christ-Wolf's head.

'They say that, like your father, you prefer your left hand for the killing stroke,' he said. His eyes as much as his voice made it a question. They were blue, to match the dawn sky, and very bright.

'Yes.' I was thinking of Einar. Of how I would tell his father. Of my mother and her warnings, and the reasons why I had not listened as I should.

'And the Saxon favoured his right?'

That was said as a question, but was not. I brought my mind back to where I was standing. Eirik Hakonson smiled, and for a moment, he looked very like the witch-man.

I said nothing. It occurred to me that I had not sworn fealty, and that the dead man was still, technically, my king. The living man was watching me. 'Eyvind Kelda tells me that your father had the sweet-water sickness, that he was already deaf and going blind, and that it pained him to walk. Is this true?'

One does not lie to one's future king. 'Yes,' I said. 'It is true.'

'It is true, is it not,' he said, absently, 'that a blow delivered by the left hand from in front, would look exactly the same as one delivered by the right hand from behind?'

I had need of water. My lips were parched to leather. I licked them, and they stayed that way. Eirik Hakonson reached behind him and gave me a water-skin. I drank and felt no better. He took it back and drank himself. His eyes searched the sky beyond my shoulder, watching the clouds to see if they were different now that he was no longer the hunted son of a murdered earl. I might have spoken then, but he put out a hand to stop me.

'I knew of your mother,' he said. 'She warned my father of his death in time for him to send me to Sweden. I have given thanks nightly to the all-father that she spoke when she did. All through the time when the Christ-Wolf was killing to enforce his new religion, I have prayed to her memory that something might be sent to stand in his way.' His eyes were really very blue. They came back to mine.

'A man who lives for the true gods might choose to make of himself a sacrifice so that the people might find their way again. This has always been so. Even the Christians have their sacrifice, albeit in their case it is the son who dies, and not the father.

73

Still, I would say that the principle is the same.'

He stood and gave me the water-skin to keep. We began to walk away from the pyre, and I saw that the entire half great-hundred of men, such as were still alive, were waiting on the far side for us to finish. The king nodded to Eyvind Kelda, who nodded back and did not smile. As we passed Einar's body, the king said; 'When you return to Orkney, you may tell your mother from me that your father did not die in vain.'